This
Shaun
the Sheep
book belongs to

....

....

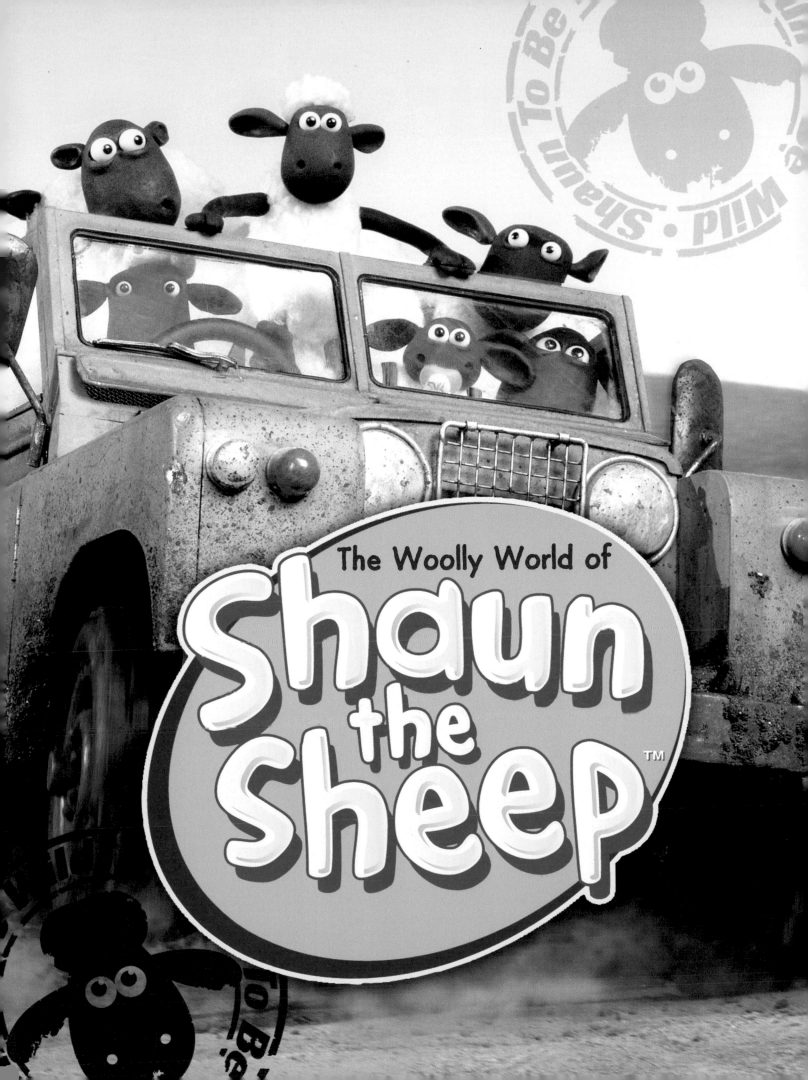

Contents

EGMONT
We bring stories to life

First Published in Great Britain 2007 by Egmont UK Limited. 239 Kensington High Street, London W8 6SA
www.egmont.co.uk

Written and edited by Brenda Apsley   Designed by Jeannette O'Toole

Based on original storylines by Sarah Ball, Ian Carney, Richard Goleszowski
and Robert Dudley, Julie Jones, Lee Pressman, Trevor Ricketts.

© and ™ Aardman Animations Ltd. 2007. All rights reserved.
Shaun the Sheep (word mark) and the character 'Shaun the Sheep' © and ™ Aardman Animations Limited.
Based upon an idea by Nick Park. Developed by Richard (Golly) Goleszowski with Alison Snowden and David Fine.

ISBN 978 1 4052 3646 1
1 3 5 7 9 10 8 6 4 2
Printed in Italy

Come and meet with

Shaun the Sheep™

Baa!

Meet

Shaun the Sheep

You think sheep are all alike: white, woolly, chewy and a bit, well, sl-o-o-o-o-o-w?
You do? Then you haven't met Shaun the sheep.

Shaun is no ordinary sheep. He's fun-loving, clever and keen, a real full-of-ideas kind of sheep. He may be young, but he's the leader of his flock, and the other sheep are always ready to join in with his want-to, what-about, why-not, let's-go, can-do ideas.

Shaun will try anything. He's not an expert, and he sometimes leaps before he looks, so he often leads the flock into tricky situations. But he always figures out a way to get them out of trouble again. There's never a dull moment when he's around. He's one of a kind!

Shaun lives on a small farm. The Farmer thinks he's in charge, but it's Shaun who really runs things. The Farmer just doesn't know it.

Shaun is ...

fearless
Up, up and awaaay!

stylish
Nice outfit, Shaun!

daring
He looks danger in the eye!

inventive
Who needs a ladder when you can call on the flock?

cool
This sheep knows how to chill!

Meet The Farmer and Bitzer

The Farmer rides around the farm on his tractor or in his jeep. He sees and hears the odd things that go on, but he doesn't know that it's Shaun and the flock who are behind them. He thinks his sheep are just … sheep. But we know different, don't we?

uh?

Ruff!

Bitzer is the Farmer's sheepdog. He wants to stay in the Farmer's good books because he wants to keep his job, so he tries to hide what's going on. Sometimes he joins in with Shaun's plans – as long as there's no chance of the Farmer finding out.

Bitzer likes tea, sandwiches and dog biscuits, listening to music and doing crosswords. He wants a quiet life, but that's the last thing he gets when Shaun's around.

Bitzer adores his girlfriend. They met when her people camped next to the sheep field. It was love at first sniff.

...and the Flock

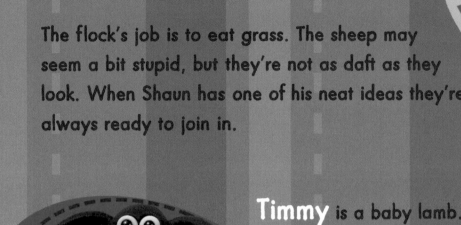

The flock's job is to eat grass. The sheep may seem a bit stupid, but they're not as daft as they look. When Shaun has one of his neat ideas they're always ready to join in.

Ba-ba!

Timmy is a baby lamb. He may look like a little angel with his dummy and teddy, but he gets into all kinds of scrapes. Find out what he did to poor Shirley on page 42.

Timmy's Mum is a bit ... distracted. She never seems to notice when Timmy misbehaves, but panics when he's in danger. She bleats, worries and wails until he's safe again.

Shirley is four times the size of a normal sheep. She's so big that she has to be pushed and pulled around. She will eat ANYTHING, as you'll find out later. She comes in handy when Shaun needs a trampoline or a battering ram. And he finds all sorts of useful stuff hidden in her king-size fleece.

Baa!

Farmyard Friends and Foes

Each morning, the **Cockerel** wakes everyone up at the crack of dawn. This does not make him the most popular bird on the farm ...

Cock-a-doodle-doo!

Shaun Is good friends with the **Duck**. Read about how he saved Shaun from an icy bath on page 24.

Quack!

The **Bull** is a huge, scary mass of muscle, as you'll see in his story, which starts on page 34. He's bad-tempered, and attacks anything red. Including red sheep ...

Roar!

Mower Mouth the goat is better known as The Eating Machine. He has no time for Shaun and the other sheep because all he thinks about is his next meal.

Hic!

Cluck!

Mother Hen and her four fluffy yellow Chicks live in the farmyard. All together now – **aaaaah!**

Three Naughty Pigs live in the sty next to the sheep field. They're cheeky, greedy, and are always arguing. They make fun of Shaun's plans, and always try their best to wreck them. On page 60 you can read what happened when they gatecrashed Shaun's disco.

Oink!

Oink!

Oink!

Scrumping

Peeep!

One morning, Bitzer had his headphones clamped to his ears when the Farmer whistled. **Peeep!** Come on.

But Bitzer just tapped his paws. Cool vibes. Chill.

"Huh!" said the Farmer, beeping his horn. **Parp-parp! PARP-PARP-PARP!**

But Bitzer didn't budge.

"Pah!" said the Farmer, throwing an apple at Bitzer's head. That did the trick!

Bitzer jumped into the back of the jeep and the Farmer drove off.

Shaun watched them go. "Baa!" he bleated. Time to top up my tan!

Baa!

14

Shaun was stretched out on a lounger when he heard noises coming from the Naughty Pigs' sty. **Munch, crunch, slurp!** They were cramming apples into their mouths. Apples from the Farmer's tree. "Oink!" they grunted. This is better than slops!

"Baa!" said Shaun. Better than grass, too! I'll get some for the flock. Shaun jumped into the sty and walked over to the Pigs. "Baaa?" he bleated, giving them a basket. Any spare apples, kind piggy friends?

"Oink?" The Naughty Pigs went into a huddle, then one of them took the basket and went off with it.

Munch,

crunch,

slurp!

When he handed it back, it was very heavy ...

Baaa?

In the sheep field, the flock was ready to picnic. But the basket was full of

rocks

pebbles

mud

slime, and

something even worse!

No apples. Not one. Not even a core.

"Tee, hee!" laughed the Naughty Pigs.

"Baa," said Shaun. It was time for Plan B.

Seconds later, sheep superhero Stilt Man appeared in the sty, wobbling and tottering towards the apple tree.

Unfortunately, his visit was a very short one. One of the Pigs used a chainsaw to cut bits off his stilts, and Stilt Man got shorter and shorter until he was Shaun-sized again.

Yeuk!

Wobble!

Bzzz!

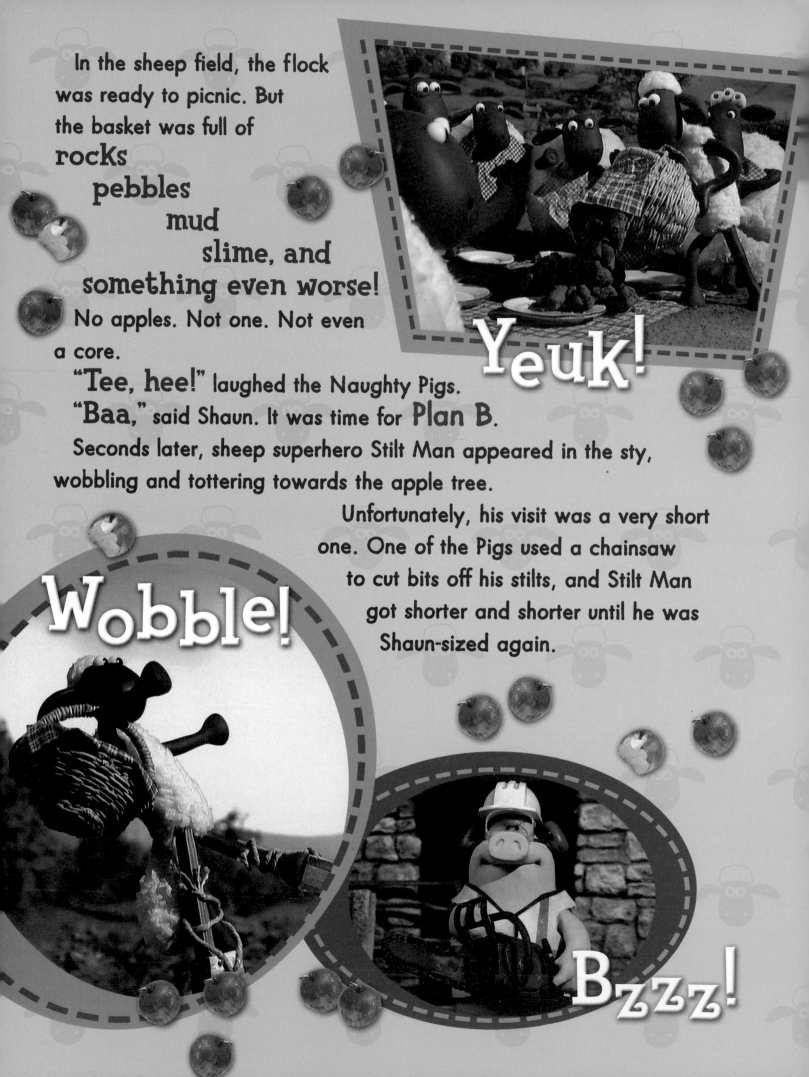

The Pigs had a game of Volleyball (you can guess who the ball was), then tossed Shaun back into the field.

"Baa," said Shaun. Plan C.

Sheep superhero Hay Bale appeared next, and shuffled towards the apple tree.

His visit was just as short, and seconds later Shaun was back in the sheep field.

"Baa!" said Shaun. If at first ... try Plan D.

The next sheep superhero, High Wire, swung into action. He fired an arrow with a rope tied to it at the apple tree, hooked an umbrella handle on the rope, and slid down it.

But the Naughty Pigs fired him straight back again.

Baaa!

Baa-aa-aaaa!

Thud!

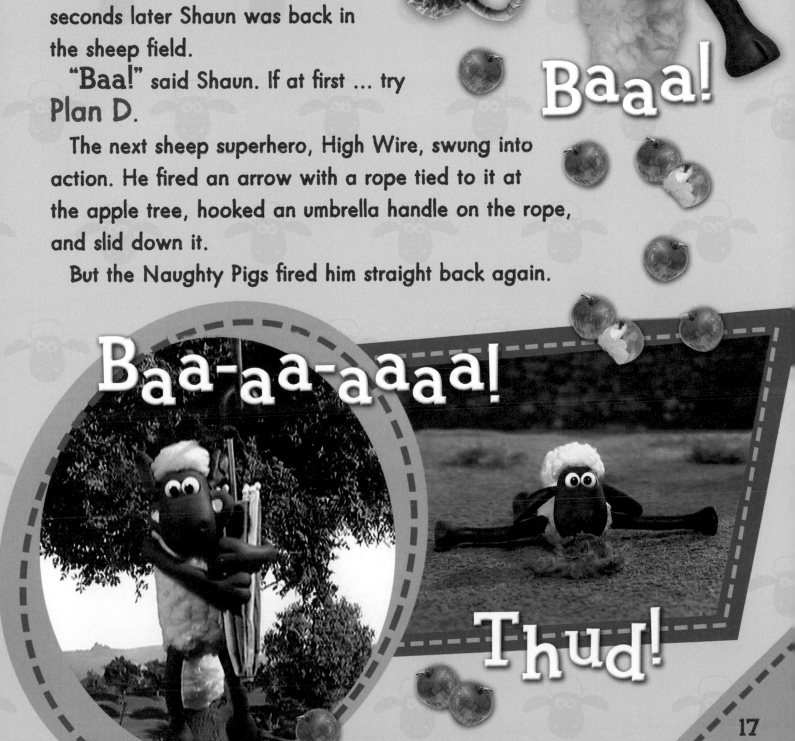

Plan E saw Shaun driving the Farmer's tractor to the back of the sty and tying a rope around the apple tree. As he drove away, the tree trunk bent, and the branches bowed low enough for Shaun to pick the apples.

Baa!

"Oink!" squealed the Naughty Pigs. Who goes there?

One of them bit through the rope and – twang! – the branches sprang back, firing hundreds of apples into the sheep field.

Twang!

Ruff?

It looked like the sky was raining apples! Hundreds of them.

When Bitzer got back, he was puzzled by the sudden appearance of the apples. "**Ruff?**" he growled. What? When? How? Who? Why?

"**Baa,**" Shaun bleated. Don't ask. Have an apple.

When the Farmer went into the Naughty Pigs' sty with a big bucket and emptied it into their trough, they took a sniff.

"**Oink-oink?**" Apples?

Wrong.

"**Yeuk!**" It was smelly, slimy, sludgy slops for tea. As usual.

Yeuk!

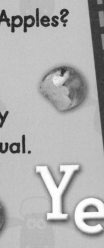

The Farmer's Apple Tree

There's always a mad scramble to get at the apples on the Farmer's tree.

Shaun built a sheep-tower with Shirley at the bottom, so he could climb up to pick the apples.

Snigger, snigger! The Naughty Pigs hid behind the tree and caught the apples in a fishing net, as Shaun threw them down. Sneaky!

But it was little Timmy who had the best idea. He sat on the grass and just **ate** the apples! "Baaaarrrp!"

Baaaarrrp!

Give Shaun a helping hoof! Can you count the apples on the tree below, and circle the number?

1 2 3 4 5 6 7 8 9 10
11 12 13 14 15 16 17 18 19 20

Colour in the picture as neatly as you can, using the colour code, then write your name on the line.

The Farmer's Apple Tree
by

....

ANSWER: There are 18 apples on the tree.

The Farmer's Tools

The Farmer's work is never done! Today he has to mend a hole in the fence to stop the sheep escaping.

"Uh?" says the Farmer. Where are his tools?

Shaun, Bitzer and the sheep rush off to find them. But they bring back all sorts of things!

"Bah!" grumbles the Farmer. Now he has another job – sorting out his tools from the other stuff!

Bah!

Can you help the Farmer?
Which are the things he **doesn't** need to mend the fence?
Write a cross ✗ in the answer box.

Bathtime

"Cock-a-doodle-dooooooo!" As usual, the Cockerel woke everyone up at dawn and the Farmer opened the big barn door.

The sheep came out, and Bitzer crossed them off on his list: Shaun, Shirley, Timmy's Mum ...

Suddenly, Bitzer's nose twitched: Smelly Sheep Alert!

"Pheeew!" he sniffed. What a pong! These sheep need a dip! Bitzer blew his whistle and pointed to the sheep-dip pool. Bathtime!

The Farmer poured a whole box of sheep-dip powder into the pool, and the sheep got ready for a day in Sheep Spa! "Baa, baa, baa!" they bleated. Sheep heaven!

Baa, baa, baa!

The Farmer turned on the blue tap and cold water gushed out. But the hot-water pipe just shook and rattled, and no water came out. "Huh!" he said, stomping off.

When the pool was full, Bitzer blew his whistle – peep-peeeep! – and pointed. Dip's ready. It was bathtime. Hurry up. You first, Shaun.

"Baa?" said Shaun, backing away. Why me? Where was the sudsy, scenty, bubbly, hot sheep-dip?

peeeeep!

This was a super-cold, icy dip. Fine for polar bears. Perfect for penguins. But not for sheep.

Just then, the Duck jumped into the pool.

The water was freezing! "Q-q-quack!" he quacked. Get me out!

Q-q-quack!

Bitzer was getting fed up. What would the Farmer say if he didn't get the sheep dipped? Something like "Su-pi da!" probably. Stupid dog!

Bitzer blew an extra-loud, sheep-ear-popping blast on his whistle – PEEEP! – and pointed to the pool. In. Now.

The flock looked at the pool, then at the frozen Duck – and ran away.

Bitzer growled. He had to stop the sheep escaping!

He looked everywhere for them, then spotted a bit of sheep behind a tree. "Ruff!" he ruffed. Gotcha!

He tiptoed to the back of the tree, and a tower of sheep shuffled to the front.

Bitzer blew his whistle – pe-pe-peep! – and the tower collapsed.

The sheep scarpered in all directions. "Bah!" said Bitzer.

Ruff!

Meanwhile, the Farmer decided he'd have a dip, too. "La-de-dah-de-dah!" he sang.

As he filled his bath, clouds of steam came out of the bathroom window.

La-de-dah-de-dah!

Shaun skidded to a stop when he saw the steam. He knew that if steam was coming out of the Farmer's bathroom, there must be hot water in there. And hot water was just what he needed ...

Shaun took the flock to the Dump. They fixed lots of bits of hosepipe together to make one long piece.

Shaun told a sheep to climb up the telegraph pole, then he pulled the hose to the Farmer's house. He gave a signal, and the sheep on the pole fixed wires to the Farmer's phone line and dialled his number.

gabble-gibble-baa-ble!

Uh?

When the Farmer answered, all he heard was **gabble-gibble-baa-ble!** **"Uh?"** he said.

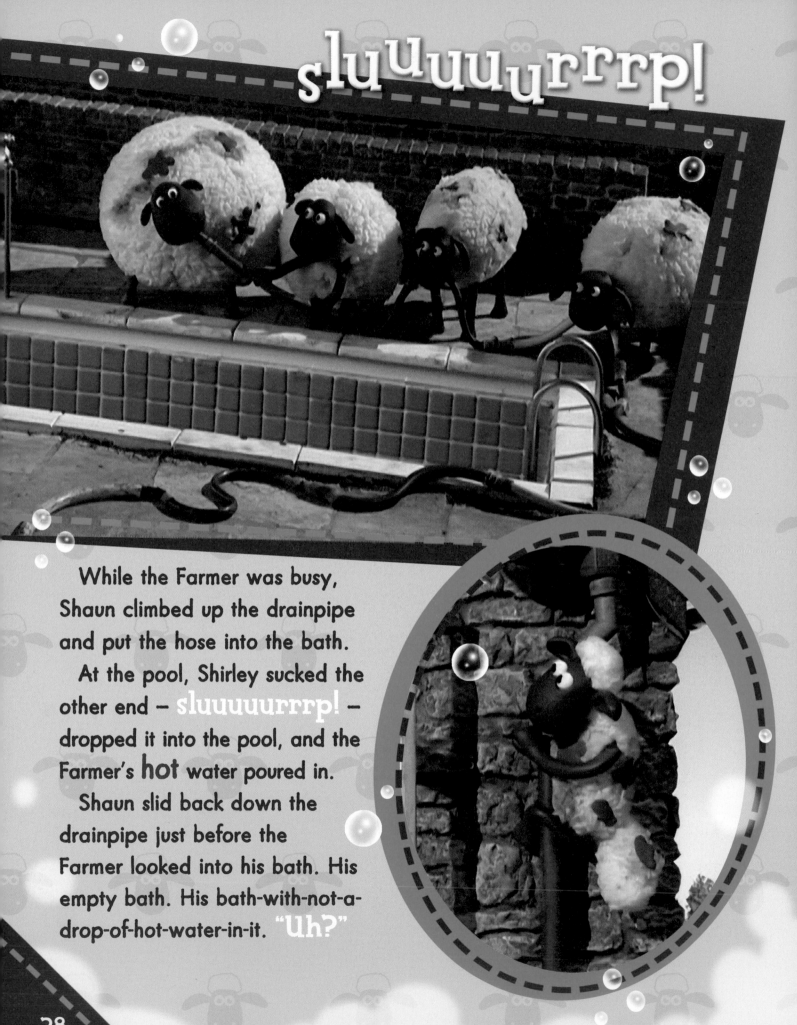

sluuuurrrp!

While the Farmer was busy, Shaun climbed up the drainpipe and put the hose into the bath.

At the pool, Shirley sucked the other end – sluuuuurrrp! – dropped it into the pool, and the Farmer's hot water poured in.

Shaun slid back down the drainpipe just before the Farmer looked into his bath. His empty bath. His bath-with-not-a-drop-of-hot-water-in-it. "Uh?"

Bitzer came back to find the sheep in the pool.

"Baaa!" said Shaun. Lovely! Sudsy! Scenty! Bubbly! Hot!

Bitzer looked around. There was no sign of the Farmer. And didn't a dog deserve a nice dip after a long day chasing smelly sheep? Yes, he did!

Bitzer and the sheep had a lovely long soak. They were still in the pool – a bit wrinkly and crinkly, but not the tiniest bit smelly – when the sun went down.

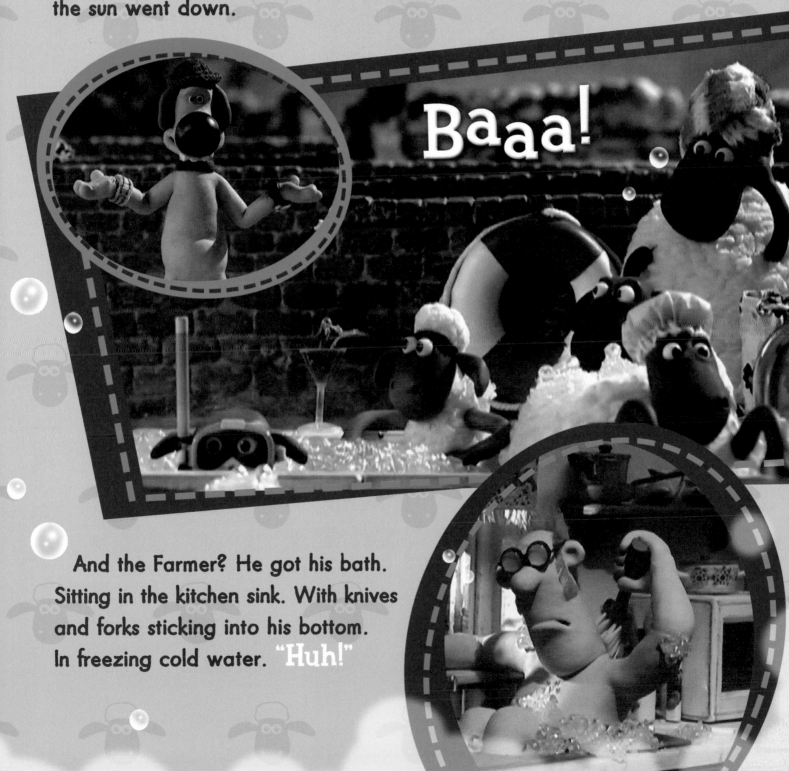

Baaa!

And the Farmer? He got his bath. Sitting in the kitchen sink. With knives and forks sticking into his bottom. In freezing cold water. "Huh!"

The Sheep Dip

The flock had a fabulous time in the sheep-dip pool — once Shaun had sorted out the little problem of the hot-water supply!

Eyes peeled! How many of these little pictures can you see in the big one? Tick ✓ a box for each one you find.

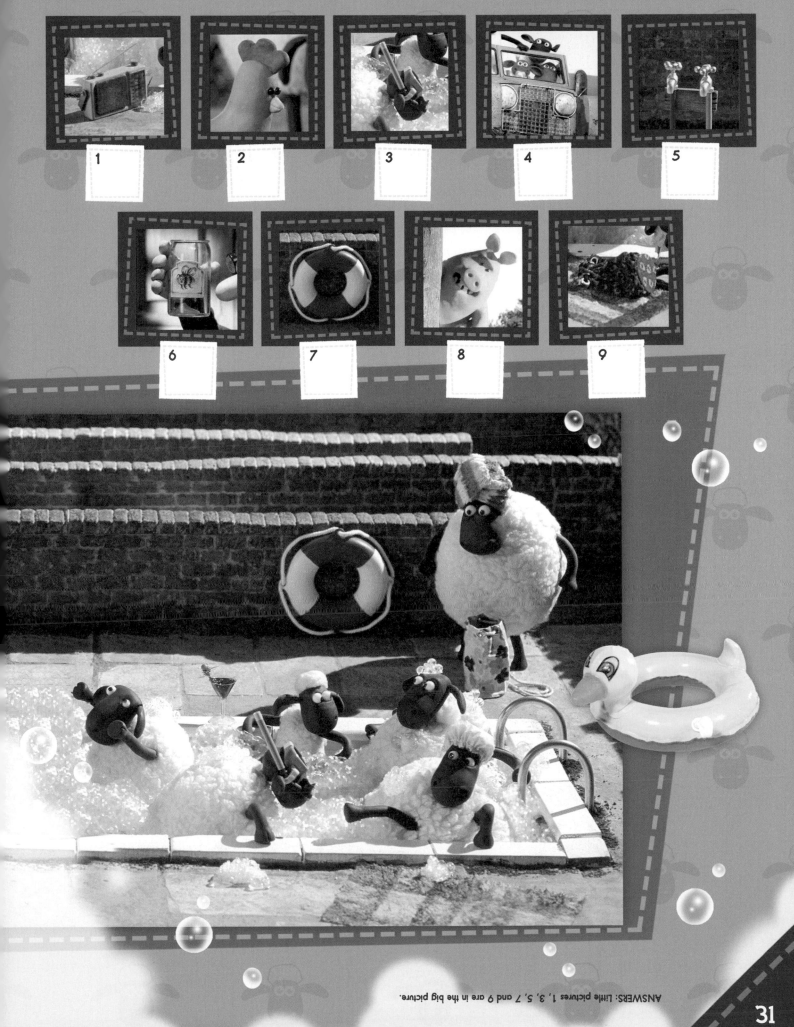

1

2

3

4

5

6

7

8

9

ANSWERS: Little pictures 1, 3, 5, 7 and 9 are in the big picture.

31

Bitzer's Puzzles

"Ruff!" Bitzer's puzzled! Can you help him find 2 pictures of Shaun that are exactly the same?

1

2

3

4

5

6

ANSWER: Pictures 2 and 6 are exactly the same.

"Ruff!" Bitzer's still puzzled. Show him which picture of Timmy is different from the rest.

1

2

3

4

5

6

The Bull

One morning, the sheep were eating breakfast. On the menu? Grass. Lots of it. As usual.

Shaun moved along, head down, teeth gnashing: chomp, chomp, chew, chew. He was so busy filling his tummy that he didn't look where he was going. Not until – bonk! – he bumped into something. He tried to push the something out of the way, but it wouldn't budge.

"Baa!" he bleated. His legs were moving, but he wasn't going anywhere …

Shaun looked up … up … and further up. The something he had bumped into was a leg. A very large leg. On top of the leg was a very large body. On top of the body was a very large neck.

Baa!

On top of the neck was a very large face. With beady eyes, flaring nostrils, and a mouth big enough to swallow Timmy in one go.

Shaun gulped. It was the Bull. And he looked angry.

"Raaooooo!" bellowed the Bull. He didn't like being pushed.

"Ba-a-a-a!" Uh-oh! Shaun was so scared that the grass he was chewing flew out and landed on the Bull's face.

"Raaooooo!" the Bull roared.

"Ba-a-a-a!" bleated Shaun, picking soggy grass off the Bull's face. Shaun took out a hanky and started to clean the Bull's nose-ring. A red hanky.

ROOOARRR!

Now Bulls hate anything red. Red jam. Timmy's red teddy. Red hanky. Red makes them angry. Very, VERY angry.

As Shaun polished, the Bull bellowed loudly – "ROOOARRR!" – and scraped the ground with a hoof, ready to charge.

"Baa ..." said Shaun.

Too late!
The Bull butted Shaun and he flew into the air.

He landed in the Naughty Pigs' sty, up to his armpits in thick, smelly mud.

"Baa!" said Shaun, stomping back to the field. That was a bit much. Time to take the Bull by the horns, Shaun thought to himself. Time to …

Baa!

RoOoARRr!

… stand shivering in his red underpants. The Bull bellowed so hard that he had blown Shaun's fleece clean off!

When Shaun bent over to pick it up, his bottom was in the Bull's eyeline. His red bottom.

The Bull charged, and Shaun flew through the air again.

You can guess where he landed. Yes, in the Naughty Pigs' sty. In the mud. Again.

When the Pigs tossed him out, the flock tidied him up. But now they were covered in mud, too.

"Ruff," growled Bitzer, pointing to the sheep-dip pool.

Shaun took a dip, then as the flock queued up, the Naughty Pigs fired a tin of paint into the pool. Red paint.

Baaaaaa!

When Bitzer got the sheep out, their fleeces were clean. But they were also red. "Ruff?" he growled. How? Who? Why?

Suddenly, he heard a loud bellow, thundering hooves, and the sound of a hundred sheep-knees knocking together. Brave Bitzer the sheepdog stood in front of his flock, blew his whistle and showed the Bull a yellow card. When the Bull just snorted, Bitzer showed him a red card. Which was not the most sensible thing to do ...

The Bull charged, and brave Bitzer ran away as fast as he could.

So did the sheep.

While the Bull chased the sheep, Bitzer and Shaun placed an order with Speedy Send Deliveries, and minutes later a big red sheet was delivered.

Off!

Shaun pretended he was a bullfighter. "**Baa!**" he bleated, flicking the sheet like a matador's cape. Over here, Señor Bullo.

The Bull charged, and Shaun whipped the sheet to one side. "**Baa!**" Missed!

Bitzer clapped. Well done!

Shaun matadored like a true ... matador, flicking the sheet this way and that as the Bull went bonkers. With a final flick, Shaun sent him crashing into the Naughty Pigs' sty. Which is where he stayed.

Later, the Farmer thought he saw red sheep in the field, and reversed back to check.

Baa!

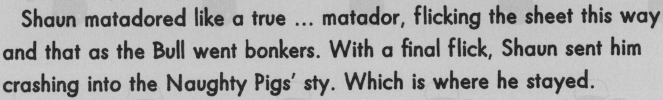

Crash!

Baa!

Luckily, Shaun had already scrubbed the back half of their fleeces clean. "**Baa!**" he bleated. Quick! The sheep turned around, so what the Farmer saw were woolly sheep bottoms. WHITE woolly sheep bottoms.

"**Baa!**" said Shaun. Phew!

Spot the Difference

It's not all hard work down on the farm. When they have a day off, Shaun and Bitzer like to go camping.

1

These pictures look the same, but there are 8 things that are different in picture 2. Binoculars at the ready! Can you spot them all?

2

ANSWERS: 1. The cooler box has changed colour; 2. Bitzer's book is missing; 3. A thermos flask and cup have appeared; 4. There are two ropes on the tent; 5. Bitzer's watch is missing; 6. One of the apples is missing; 7. A deckchair has appeared; 8. The radio is missing.

41

Shape Up with Shaun

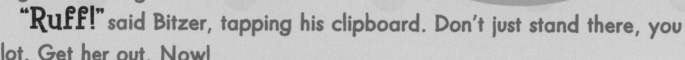

Every morning is the same for Bitzer. He ticks off the sheep on his list as they come out of the barn.

But this morning, something was different. There was one sheep not crossed off on his list. Shirley was too big to fit through the barn door.

"Ruff!" said Bitzer, tapping his clipboard. Don't just stand there, you lot. Get her out. Now!

Shaun squeezed Shirley into a shopping trolley and wheeled her out into the field. But it was hard work. She was very big.

"Baa?" bleated Shaun. Just how heavy WAS Shirley? He put a plank across an oil drum and fixed Shirley's shopping trolley to one end. Then he fixed another trolley to the other end of the plank, like a see-saw, and started to put bricks into it.

Baa?

Shaun put in 10 bricks. Then more. And more. And more. 20 bricks, 21, 22, 23, 24, 25, 26. It wasn't until Shaun added brick number 27 that Shirley lifted off the ground and the see-saw was level.

Baa!

"**Baa!**" said Shaun, writing a sum on the blackboard:

Shirley = 27 bricks

Shirley was too heavy. She had to lose some weight and to do that she first had to get active. Shaun was the sheep to help her!

First, he showed Shirley how to skip. But the skipping rope wasn't long enough to go around Shirley, so Shaun used the Farmer's washing line instead. Complete with washing. Underpants. Vests. Long johns.

Shirley did try hard, but she just wasn't very good at skipping, and instead of jumping over the rope she jumped into the Farmer's blue vest, and his underpants ended up on her head. "**Baa!**" she said. I like this stuff!

"**Baa!**" said Shaun. Let's try the hay-baling treadmill.

Question: How to get Shirley to get on it?

Answer: Tie a bun to a string on the end of a pole and dangle it in front of her. Sorted.

Baa!

After a few days of his Let's-Get-Shirley-Slim Exercise Plan, Shaun weighed Shirley again. This time he had to take out one brick to make the see-saw balance. **"Baa!"** said Shaun. Good. She was getting lighter!

He wrote a new sum on the blackboard:

Shirley = 26 bricks

Shaun made Shirley sweat. She did

tractor-tyre training ...

Go!

sheep-lifting ...

Go!

and even
pumpkin-boxing.

Go!

Then Shaun showed Shirley what to eat (not a lot) ... and what NOT to eat (almost everything).

Shaun's Let's-Get-Shirley-Slim Exercise Plan went on working, and every day there was a little less of Shirley.

Each time he weighed her, Shaun needed fewer bricks – 25, 24, 23, 22, 21, 20, 19, 18, 17, 16, 15 – until one day he wrote on the blackboard:

Shirley = 14 bricks

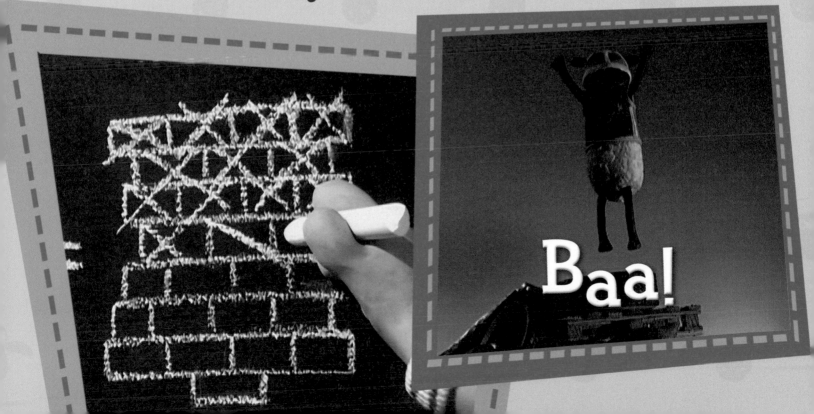

At Shirley's next weigh-in, Timmy's Mum brought the bricks in the Farmer's tractor, as usual. But naughty Timmy pulled a lever, and the bricks fell into the empty shopping trolley. All of them. Hundreds.

Baaaaaa!

Aaarrgh!

When the bricks landed in the trolley, (Slimline) Shirley flew up into the air, across the field and over a hedge.

She was on her way down again when her fall was broken by a truck. A big truck. A big pie truck. A big pie truck full of big fruit pies.

She crashed through the side, sniffed — and found herself in Shirley Heaven.

Shaun found her by following the **munch-munch** sounds coming from the back of the pie truck. And the smell of pies. **"Baa!"** he said. Uh-oh!

munch!

munch-
munch!

By the time Shaun climbed inside, Shirley had eaten so many pies, she had grown back to her normal size: big.

The other sheep smelled the pies, jumped into the truck and –

munch-slurp-munch! –
ate the ones Shirley hadn't eaten.

Now the whole flock was big.

Shaun had to get the sheep slim again, and that's how Shaun's Slim-and-Shapely-Sheep Exercise Class began.

The whole flock joined in … even Shirley!

Baa!

Baa!

Work it!

Shapely Sheep

The sheep were too big by the time they had munched their way through all those pies in the pie truck.

There was only one thing for it. Personal trainer Shaun put on his stripy headband, played loud disco music, and Shaun's Slim-and-Shapely-Sheep Exercise Class began.

"**Baa!**" said Shaun. Work those hooves! Step. Kick. Step. Kick ...

Which 4 pieces are missing from the jigsaw puzzle picture?
Draw and colour them in if you like.

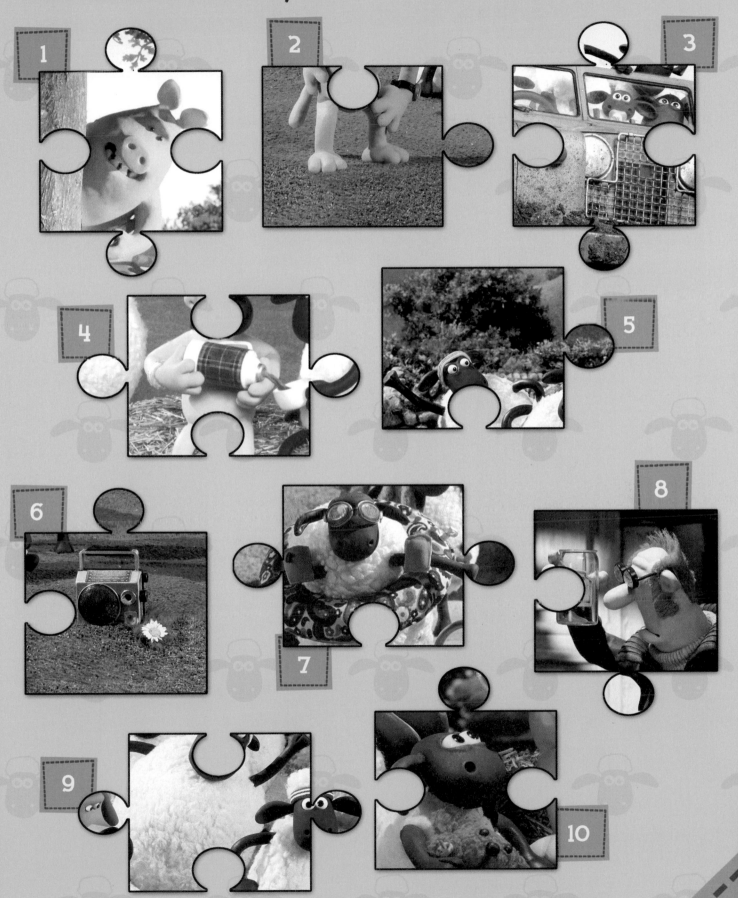

Bitzer's Bits and Pieces

Every day is a busy day for Bitzer. He gets up when the Cockerel crows at dawn, and his first job is to check off the sheep on his list when the Farmer lets them out of the barn.

There's always something for Bitzer to do. He spends his day:

catching runaway sheep ...

blowing his whistle ...

being nice to the Farmer ...

keeping his hat on ...

trying to work out what Shaun is up to ...

scratching and sniffing!

The only time Bitzer stops is when it's time for a little sit down, a sandwich, a dog biscuit or three, and a cup of tea. "Aaaaah!"

What does Bitzer need? Which of these bits and pieces does he take with him every morning?
Tick ✔ **the boxes.**

1

2

3

4

5

6

7

8

9

10

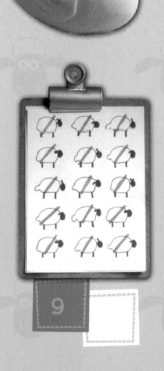

Off the Baaa!

Shaun was bored. "Baa," he yawned. Life on the farm was not always very exciting.

Shaun was wrong! Seconds later, something VERY exciting happened. Exciting for the Farmer, but dangerous for the Duck, when he waddled out in front of the Farmer's tractor!

"Uh?" said the Farmer, swerving so hard that a big cabbage flew out of the trailer.

Screech!

Quack!

It sailed through the air, landed in the sheep field, and rolled up to Shaun. "Baa!" he bleated. That's more like it.

He held the cabbage, turned it this way and that, shook it, rubbed it, sniffed it – and licked it. "Yeuk!" It tasted just like, er, cabbage.

Yeuk!

52

Shaun rolled the cabbage with his hoof, kicked it, then headed it. He bounced if off his knee, his head, his nose, then balanced it on the back of his neck.

"Baa!" he said. This is no ordinary cabbage. It's a football-cabbage!

Now it takes a lot to distract the flock from chewing grass, but Shaun's keepy-uppies did the trick.

"Oooooooh!" they said, clapping their hooves. Nifty hoof-work!

Shaun kicked the ball and – boing! boing! – the flock headed it from sheep to sheep. They were good. "Baa!" said Shaun. Match time!

But before they could have a match, Shaun needed to make a goal. No problem. Easy peasy. Here's how:

1. Pile three sheep, one on top of the other.
2. Pile up another three.
3. Cut down a signpost.
4. Put the signpost between the piles of sheep to make a crossbar.

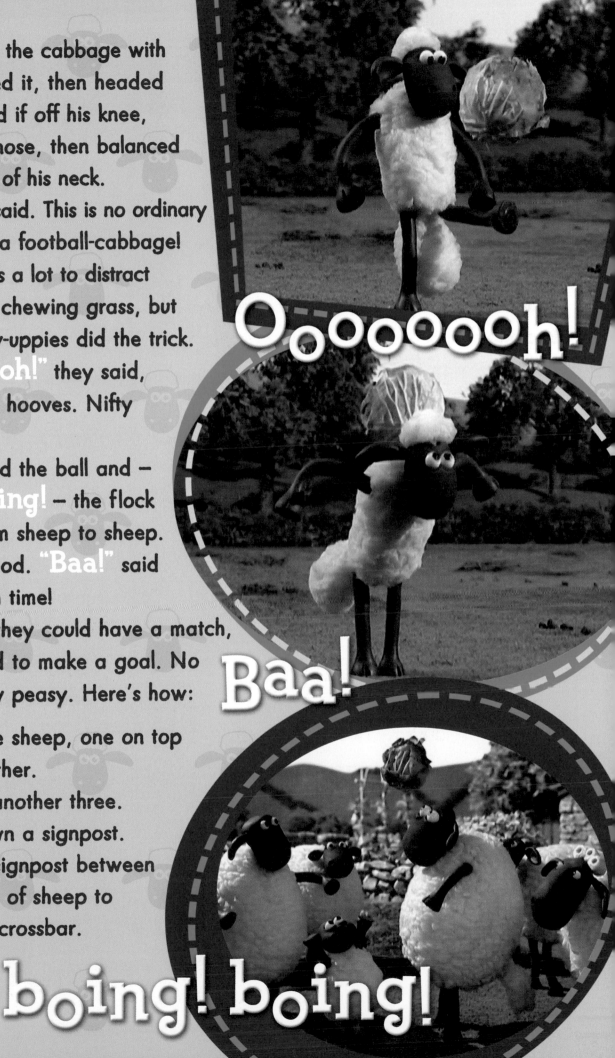

Oooooooh!

Baa!

boing! boing!

Shaun thought hard about who should be goalkeeper.

Then he had an idea: Timmy's Mum, because she was the only sheep who owned a pair of gloves. Even if they were flowery oven gloves!

But who to choose as referee?

Shaun knew just who it should be! Bitzer, because he was the only one with a whistle.

When he blew it – peeeep! – the big match kicked off. The Naughty Pigs had their eyes on the football-cabbage.

Peeep!

Not because they liked footie. No, they liked cabbage, and planned to eat it!

They fired a rubber sink plunger tied to a piece of rope at the cabbage. But what they pulled into the sty wasn't the cabbage – it was Bitzer's nose, followed by an angry Bitzer!

"Grrrrrr!" he growled. Ged dis ding off by dose! Dow!

Oink!

Grrrr!

54

Smash!

Baa!

Tinkle!

Bitzer restarted the game, but – smash! tinkle! – one of the sheep kicked the cabbage through a window in the Farmer's house.

"Baa!" said the sheep. Hide!

"Ruff!" said Bitzer, pointing at one of them. Go get it!

Seconds later – smash! tinkle! – the football-cabbage flew out through another window. Another broken window.

"Ruff!" growled Bitzer.

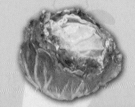

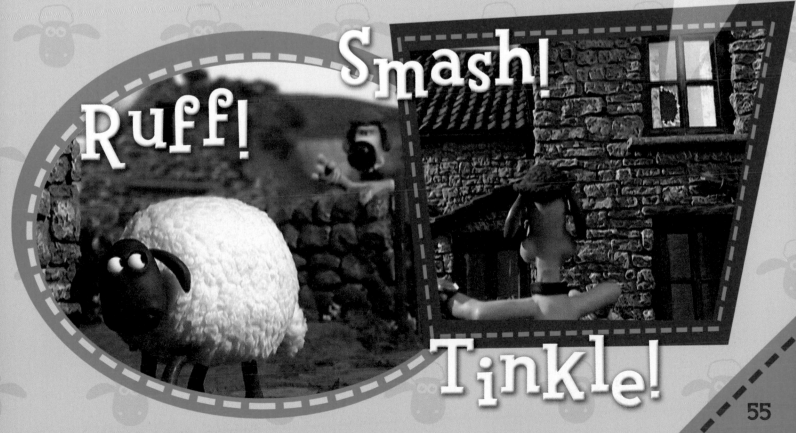

Ruff!

Smash!

Tinkle!

Shaun got the cabbage, and was heading for goal when big Shirley flattened him.

Referee Bitzer took out his red card. "Ruff!" he said. Off!

Then he pointed to the spot. Penalty!

Shaun kicked the cabbage as hard as he could. It flew towards Timmy's Mum, went over her head, then under the baaa! **Goooooool!**

The cabbage landed in the Naughty Pigs' sty and Shaun went to get it. "Baa?" he bleated. Can we have our ball back?

"Oink!" grunted the Naughty Pigs, their tongues hanging out. No way.

Oink!

Shaun worked out a plan. The flock made a tall woolly tower and lowered him into the sty, where he grabbed the cabbage just as the Pigs were about to eat it.

But one Pig held on to the cabbage, and pulled so hard that the sheep tower fell down.

Baa!

Oink!

Shaun flew into the air. So did the Pig. And so did the cabbage. Which is when the second exciting thing happened. To the Duck. Again. He opened his beak – Quaaack! – and swallowed the cabbage! The whole thing.

Shaun had a soft landing in Shirley's fleece. "Baa?" he said, as the Duck flew unsteadily overhead. Can we have our ball back, please?

Quaaack!

Baa?

Counting Fun

When the Farmer's not around, Bitzer and Shaun like going off for a picnic. It's time to read comics and listen to music. The only trouble is, you can bet your last sheep pellet that when it's time to take out the dog food and grass sandwiches, lots of guests will turn up. Hungry guests.

Count the things in the picture, then circle a number for each set.

a.	pigs	1	2	3	4	5
b.	chickens	1	2	3	4	5
c.	flasks	1	2	3	4	5
d.	flowers	1	2	3	4	5
e.	apples	1	2	3	4	5
f.	sheep	1	2	3	4	5

ANSWERS: a. 3; b. 1; c. 1; d. 5; e. 2; f. 4, including Shaun.

Saturday Night Shaun

Ding, dong! One Saturday morning, the postman arrived with a new super-duper hi-tech music system for the Farmer. It had all kinds of dials and buttons and lights and gizmos. There were wires poking out all over the place – and lots of holes to fit them into.

Ah?

"**Ah?**" said the Farmer, scratching his head. Where do this lot go?

The Farmer took his old record player and records to the Dump. Which is where Shaun and the flock found them.

Baa?

Baa?

Now Shaun's not daft, and when he found the plug, he knew just what to do with it. While the other sheep used the Farmer's old records as frisbees, he went into the barn and plugged it into a socket.

"**Ba-ba!**" said Timmy, and his mum sat him on the turntable.

Shaun flicked a switch and the turntable started to turn.

Round and round it went. Round and round went Timmy.

The turntable turned faster and faster. So did Timmy. Until he flew off ...

Ba-a-a-a!

The Farmer was still trying to get his new music system working when he heard ... music! "**Ah,**" he said. Easy-peasy!

The Farmer didn't know it, but the music wasn't coming from his system. It was coming from the sheep field, where Shaun had worked out how to play his old records.

Shaun took the record player into the barn and set it up on an old chest covered with silver foil. Then he put up strings of fairy lights and hung a big, shiny glitterball from the roof. Disco time!

That night, the sounds of DJ Shaun and his Saturday Night Disco filled the barn.

The flock watched as Shaun showed off his disco moves.

"**Baa! Baa!**" Cool! Snake hips!

Cool!

Baa!

Baa!

Baa!

In the house, the Farmer tried — and failed — to get his new music system working. **"Pah!"** he said. New-fangled rubbish!

The Farmer took it to the Dump. Which is where Shirley found it, while out searching for a late-night snack. Something tasty like an old mop, a dustbin lid — or this silvery, shiny thingy, which she nudged, sniffed — and swallowed!

Sniff!

Back at the disco, Bitzer was in charge of the guest list. The sheep were all on it … but the Naughty Pigs weren't. Even if they were wearing stripy headbands and medallions. **"Ruff!"** he said, holding out his paw. No Pigs Allowed.

Oink?

Ruff!

The Naughty Pigs grunted — and sneaked in through the side door instead.

The Pigs shoved Shaun out of the way with a flick of their hips, and started playing music they liked. Loud music. Electro-techno-pig-rap.

Then the Pigs showed off their break-dancing skills. Unfortunately, they didn't have any dancing skills. They did, however, have breaking skills, as one of them showed when he spun around on his head, went out of control, and crashed into Shaun's deck, knocking it to the floor. The record player smashed into pieces!

Crash! **Smash!**

Shaun sighed, took down the fairy lights and the glitterball, and put them in a shopping trolley with the bits of record player.

"**Baa!**" That's the end of Shaun's Saturday Night Disco, Shaun thought to himself.

Or was it?

Next morning, Shaun got to the Dump just as Shirley arrived.

When she opened her mouth to say hello, music came out – disco music! The Farmer's new music system was in her tummy, working perfectly!

"**Baa!**" said Shaun, shaking his hips. Do that again. Shirley opened her mouth, and music came out again. "**Ba-ba-ba-ba, ba-ba-ba-ba, ba-ba-ba!**"

Baa!

Shaun had an idea. He told Shirley to stand on a hay bale, then he set up a microphone for her.

"**Ba-ba-ba-ba, ba-ba-ba-ba, ba-ba-ba!**" sang Shirley.

"**Ba-ba-ba-ba, ba-ba-ba-ba, ba-ba-ba!**" sang the sheep, as they swayed from side to side. Shaun and his Saturday Night (now Sunday Morning) Disco were back in action. Featuring special guest, Shirley the Singing Sheep.

"**Ba-ba-ba-baaaa!**" sang Shirley.

Ba-ba-ba-baaaa!

DJ Shaun's Disco

When Shaun turned the barn into his Saturday Night Disco, he spun some groovy sounds on the Farmer's old record player. What a DJ! What a mover! What a star!

How many stars can you see in the picture above?
Colour in an outline for each one, then write the number.

How many fairy lights?
Colour in an outline for each one, then write the number.

ANSWERS: There are 12 stars and 8 fairy lights.

Here's a poster of DJ Shaun in action. Colour it in as neatly as you can. Use the picture as a guide or choose your own colours.

Shaun's Quiz

How much do you know about Shaun and the farm?

1
How many **Naughty Pigs** live in the Farmer's yard?

Oink!

2
What **colour** is **Timmy's** teddy?

3
What is the name of this **big sheep**?

4
The Farmer rides around on a **bike**.

True ✔   False ✗

Huh?

68

5

Who **wakes** Bitzer and the others **every morning?**

6

At the start of **Shape Up with Shaun** on page 42, how many bricks did Shirley weigh? Was it
a. 7   b. 17, or c. 27?

7

What **colour** is Bitzer's **woolly hat?** Is it red or blue?

Ruff!

8

Mower Mouth is a goat.

True ✓   False ✗

9

In **Bathtime** on page 24, who jumped into the sheep-dip pool before the sheep?

10

How many **rollers** does Timmy's Mum wear in her **hair?**

Ba-ba!

ANSWERS: 1. 3; 2. Red; 3. Shirley; 4. False, he has a Jeep and a tractor; 5. The Cockerel; 6. c; 27; 7. Blue; 8. True; 9. The Duck; 10. 3.

69